Mother, May I?

Mother, May I?

Grace Maccarone

Illustrated by
Melissa Sweet

SCHOLASTIC INC.
New York Toronto London Auckland Sydney
Mexico City New Delhi Hong Kong Buenos Aires

Mother, may I go outside?

Mother, will we
walk or ride?

May I get inside the car?

Mother, are we going far?

Now that we are at the mall,
may I buy a basketball?

Or, Mother, may I have this toy?
It's a toy I would enjoy.

Mother, may I have a treat —
something cold and smooth and sweet?

Oh, Mother, may I have a pet?
A pet would be the best thing yet —

a parakeet,

a snake,

a guppy,

a guinea pig,

a mouse,

a puppy!

Mother, may I
have some money
for a kitty
or a bunny?

On second thought,
forget the rest.
This is just my one request.
Mother, may I have a hug?

And,
Mother,
may I
keep this bug?

To Jordan —G.M.

ISBN-13: 978-0-439-92401-6
ISBN: 0-439-92401-4

12 11 10 9 8 7 6 5 4 3 2 1   7 8 9 10 11 12/0

Printed in U.S.A.
First Scholastic paperback printing, May 2007